Earwig
and the
Witch

DIANA WYNNE JONES

Earwig
and the
Witch

ILLUSTRATED BY
PAUL O. ZELINSKY

Greenwillow Books
An Imprint of HarperCollinsPublishers

Earwig and the Witch
Text copyright © 2012 by The Estate of Diana Wynne Jones
Illustrations copyright © 2012 by Paul O. Zelinsky
First published in hardcover in 2012; first Greenwillow paperback edition, 2014;
movie tie-in paperback edition, 2021.

The text of this book is set in Times New Roman.
Book design by Sylvie Le Floc'h

Library of Congress Cataloging-in-Publication Data

Jones, Diana Wynne.
Earwig and the witch / by Diana Wynne Jones ; [illustrator, Paul O. Zelinsky].
p. cm.
"Greenwillow Books."
Summary: Although an orphan, Earwig has always enjoyed living at St. Morwald's, where she manages to make everyone do her bidding, but when she is taken in by foster parents who are actually a witch and a demon, she has a hard time trying to turn the situation to her advantage.
ISBN 978-0-06-207511-6 (trade bdg.)—ISBN 978-0-06-207513-0 (pbk.)
—ISBN 978-0-06-313652-6 (movie tie-in pbk.)
[1. Orphans—Fiction. 2. Witches—Fiction. 3. Magic—Fiction. 4. Cats—Fiction.]
I. Zelinsky, Paul O., ill. II. Title.
PZ7.J684Ear 2011   [Fic]—dc22   2010048999

21 22 23 24 25 PC/LSCH 10 9 8 7 6 5 4 3 2

 Greenwillow Books

Earwig
and the
Witch

Chapter 1

At St. Morwald's Home for Children it was the day when people who wanted to be foster parents came to see which children they might want to take home with them.

"How *boring*!" Earwig said to her friend Custard. The two of them were lined up in the dining room with the bigger children. Earwig thought this whole afternoon was an utter waste of time. She was perfectly happy at St. Morwald's. She liked the clean smell of polish everywhere and the bright, sunny rooms. She liked the people there. This was because everyone, from Mrs. Briggs the Matron to the newest and smallest children, did exactly what Earwig wanted. If Earwig fancied shepherd's pie for lunch, she could get the cook to make it for her. If she wanted a new red sweater, Mrs. Briggs hurried out and bought it for her. If she wanted to play hide-and-seek in the dark, all the children played, even though some of them were frightened. Earwig was never frightened. She had a very strong personality.

There were noises from the playroom next door, where the babies and toddlers were lined up, too. Earwig could hear people crying out, "Oh, isn't she sweet!" and "Oh, just look at this little one's *eyes*!"

"Disgusting!" Earwig muttered. "What cheek!" Earwig liked most of the babies and all the toddlers, but she did not think they were made to be admired. They were people, not dolls.

"It's all right for you," her friend Custard said. "Nobody ever chooses you."

Earwig liked Custard best out of everyone at St. Morwald's. He always did exactly what she said. His only fault was that he got scared rather

too often. She said soothingly, "You never get chosen either. Don't worry."

"But people hover over me," Custard said. "Sometimes they *almost* choose me." Then he added, very daringly, "Don't you ever want to be chosen and go to live somewhere else, Earwig?"

"No," Earwig said firmly. But she wondered about it. Might it just be fun to go and live in an ordinary house the way other children did? Then she thought of all the numbers of people in St. Morwald's who all did exactly what she wanted, and she realized that in an ordinary house, there would only be two or three people, or six at the most. That was far too few to be interesting. "No," she said.

"Anyone who chose me would have to be very unusual."

Just then, Mrs. Briggs came hurrying through from the playroom, looking flustered. "The bigger ones are in here," she said. "If you'd like to follow me, I'll tell you the names and a little bit about each child."

Earwig had only time to whisper warningly to Custard, "Remember to cross your eyes like I taught you!" before a very strange couple followed Mrs. Briggs into the dining room. Earwig could see that they had tried to make themselves look ordinary, but she knew they were not, not in the least. The woman had one brown eye and one blue one, and a raggety, ribby look to her face. It was not a nice face. The woman had tried to make it nicer by doing her hair in blue-rinsed curls and putting on a lot of purple lipstick. This did not go with her brown tweed suit or her bright green sweater. And none of it went with her big red hat or her sky-blue high-heeled boots.

As for the man—the first time Earwig looked at him, he looked like anyone you might pass in the street. The second time she looked, she could hardly see him at all. He was like a long black streak in the air. After that, every time she looked at the man, he seemed taller, and taller still, and his face seemed grimmer and more frowning. And he seemed to have long ears. By the time the man and the woman were standing in front of

Custard, Earwig was almost sure that the man was nine feet tall and that he *did* have two somethings sticking up from his head. The somethings could have been ears, but Earwig rather thought they were horns.

"This little boy is John Coster," Mrs. Briggs was saying. Earwig was glad she was not Custard. "His parents were both killed in a fire," Mrs. Briggs explained. "So sad!"

Custard usually scowled when Mrs. Briggs said this kind of thing. He hated people

saying his life was sad. But Earwig could see he was so frightened of the strange couple that he could not even frown. And he had quite forgotten to cross his eyes.

Before Earwig could nudge Custard to remind him to cross his eyes, the strange couple lost interest in him. They moved on to stand in front of Earwig. Custard went white with relief.

Mrs. Briggs sighed. "And this is Erica Wigg," she said hopelessly. Mrs. Briggs never could quite pin down just why it was that nobody ever wanted to take Earwig home with them. Earwig was skinny. Her front teeth and her elbows stuck out rather, and she insisted on doing her hair in two bunches that stuck out, too, just like her elbows and her teeth. But Mrs. Briggs had known far worse-looking children who seemed to be wanted by everyone. What Mrs. Briggs did not know was that Earwig was very good at making herself look unlovable. It was something that she did quite quietly, on the inside of her face, and she always did it, because she was quite happy to stay at St. Morwald's.

She made herself look unlovable now. She thought these two people were the most awful she had ever seen. They stared at her grimly.

"Erica has been with us since she was a baby," Mrs. Briggs said brightly, seeing the way they were looking. She did not say, because she always

11

thought it was so peculiar, that Earwig had been left on the doorstep of St. Morwald's early one morning with a note pinned to her shawl. The note said:

GOT THE OTHER TWELVE WITCHES ALL CHASING ME. I'LL BE BACK FOR HER WHEN I'VE SHOOK THEM OFF. IT MAY TAKE YEARS. HER NAME IS EARWIG.

The Matron and the Assistant Matron scratched their heads over this. The Assistant Matron said, "If this mother's one of thirteen, she must be a witch who has annoyed the rest of her coven."

"Nonsense!" said the Matron.

"But," said the Assistant Matron, "this means that the baby could be a witch as well."

Matron said "Nonsense!" again. "There are no such things as witches."

Mrs. Briggs had never told Earwig about the note, nor that her name really *was* Earwig. She thought it was probably a bad joke. Earwig was not a real name. Mrs. Briggs had written "Erica Wigg" firmly on Earwig's birth certificate and kept her mouth shut about the rest.

Meanwhile, Earwig was making herself look as unlovable as she could. Custard was edging away from her and even Mrs. Briggs was thinking what a pity it was that Earwig's charming nature never seemed to show when it mattered. And the strange couple was looking as if they thought Earwig was quite hateful.

The woman turned to the nine-foot man and looked up at him from under her red hat.

"Well?" she said. "What does the Mandrake think?"

"I think probably," he answered in a deep, angry voice.

The woman turned to Mrs. Briggs. "We'll take this one," she said, just as if Earwig were a melon or a joint of meat on the market.

Mrs. Briggs was so surprised that she rocked

back on her feet. Before she could recover, Earwig said, "No she won't. I want to stay here."

"Don't be silly, dear," said Mrs. Briggs. "You know how much everyone here wants to see you living with a real family, just like other children."

"I don't want to," said Earwig. "I want to stay with Custard."

"Now, dear," said Mrs. Briggs. "These kind people live quite near, in Lime Avenue. I'm sure they'll let you come back to see your friends whenever you want to, and when school starts again you'll be able to see Custard every day."

After that, there seemed nothing Earwig could do but go and help one of the trainee girls pack her things in a bag, while Mrs. Briggs took the strange couple to her office to sign forms. Then she had to say good-bye to Custard and hurry after the woman in the red hat and the nine-foot man. The things on his head *were* horns, Earwig was sure. She was surprised nobody else noticed. But mostly she was angry and amazed that, for the first time in her life, somebody was making her do something she didn't want to do. She could not understand it.

I suppose I'd better think of it as a challenge, she said to herself as they turned in to Lime Avenue.

Chapter 2

Earwig was not at all surprised to find that the house in Lime Avenue was Number Thirteen. It fitted these people, even if it was only a perfectly ordinary bungalow. The nine-foot man opened the gate and went through a neat garden with diamond-shaped rose beds in the exact center of

each lawn. The windows of the bungalow were all nice and low, Earwig noticed. They would be easy to climb out of if the challenge got too much for her and she decided to run away.

The man went through the front door first and walked away down the hall, saying, "I got you what you wanted. Now I don't want to be disturbed anymore."

Earwig did not see where he went then, because the woman opened the nearest door on the right and slung Earwig's bag inside it. "You'll be sleeping in there," she said. Earwig had just a glimpse of a small bare bedroom before the woman shut the door and took her big red hat off. As she hung it carefully on a peg, she said, "Now let's get a few things straight. My name is Bella Yaga and I am a witch. I've brought you here because I need another pair of hands. If you work hard and do what you're told like a good girl, I shan't do anything to hurt you. If—"

Earwig saw that this was going to be a very big challenge indeed, far bigger than any she had faced at St. Morwald's. That was all right. She liked a challenge. And somewhere at the back of her mind, Earwig had always hoped that perhaps one day she might find a person who could teach her some magic. "That's all right," she interrupted. If you want to make somebody do what you want, it is very important to start with them in the right way. Earwig knew all about that. "It's all right," she said. "I didn't think you looked like a foster mother. So it's settled, then. You agree to teach me magic and I agree to stay here and be your assistant."

She could tell Bella Yaga had expected to have to bully and threaten her. "Well, that's settled, then," she said crossly. She looked quite put out. "You'd better come in here and start work." She led Earwig through the door on the left.

Earwig looked around and tried not to sniff too loudly. She had never seen a place so dirty. Since she was used to the airy rooms and clean polished floors of St. Morwald's, it was quite a shock. Everything was covered with dust. There was a kind of sludge on the floor made of old dirt, green mold, and the remains of spells—which mostly seemed to be little white bones and small black rotting things. The sludge rose to a hill in one corner, on which perched a rusty black cauldron with green flames flickering under it. The smell of burning was awful. More smelly things like dusty bottles and old brown packets lay about, some of them spilling, on the long dirty table, or were chucked higgledy-piggledy on the shelves. All the bowls and jugs stacked on the floor were covered with grime or brown slime.

Earwig closed her nose against the smell, wondering if witchcraft really *needed* so many rotting things. She thought that,

when she had learned enough, she would be a new kind of witch, a clean one. Meanwhile, she looked around the room and was puzzled to see that it seemed to be at least the size of the whole bungalow.

Bella Yaga chuckled at the look on Earwig's face. "Come along, girl," she said. "You're not here to stare. If you don't like it, you can clean it later. For now, I want you at this table, powdering those rats' bones for me." When Earwig came over to the table, getting her ankles tangled with two dead snakes on the way, Bella Yaga said, "Now, there's one great rule in this house. You must learn it straightaway. You must on no account *ever* disturb the Mandrake."

"You mean the man with the horns?" Earwig said.

"He hasn't got horns!" Bella Yaga said angrily. "At least, most of the time he hasn't. He gets those when he's disturbed."

"What else happens when he's disturbed?" Earwig asked.

She thought Bella Yaga shuddered at the idea. "Awful things," she said. "If you're lucky, you won't find out. Now get to work."

Soon Earwig was pounding away with a heavy pestle in a little stone bowl. At first the small white bones in the bowl went *crunch, crunch*. After an hour, they were white powder and went *spluff, spluff*, but Bella Yaga said the

27

powder had to be finer than the finest flour and she made Earwig go on pounding. By this time, Earwig's arms ached and she was bored. Bella Yaga would not tell her why she was having to make the powder. She would not answer any of Earwig's questions at all.

Earwig saw quite clearly that Bella Yaga was not going to teach her magic. She just wanted Earwig to do the hard work. Earwig knew she would have to do something about that, as soon as she knew enough about Bella Yaga and her bungalow and all her ways. So Earwig went on pounding at the powder and kept her eyes and ears open.

The only other living creature in the workroom

was a black cat, who spent his time lurking
miserably in the warmth behind the rusty
cauldron. Every so often Bella Yaga would run
her finger down a page of the greasy little book
on the table beside her and mutter, "Calls for a
familiar here." Then she would march over to the
cauldron shouting, "Come on, Thomas! Time to
do your stuff!"

Thomas always tried to escape. Once Bella Yaga caught him with only a short scuffle, but most times he fled around the walls of the room with Bella Yaga pounding after him, bawling, "Do what you're told, Thomas, or I shall give you worms!" When she caught Thomas, she marched back to the table carrying him by the scruff of his neck and dumped him beside the greasy book. Thomas crouched there in an angry ruffled heap until Bella Yaga had finished that part of her spell. Then he fled back behind the cauldron again.

Earwig could see that the greasy book had all Bella Yaga's spells in it. From where Earwig stood, it reminded her of the book of recipes the cook at St. Morwald's kept, except that this

book was a lot dirtier. The third time Bella Yaga
went pounding around the room after Thomas,
Earwig kept hammering away at the powder with
one hand and pulled the little book nearer with the
other hand. Still banging away one-handed, she
turned the pages.

"A Spell to Win First Prize in a Dog Show"

was the one Bella Yaga was working on at the moment. The next page was "To Make Next-Door Dahlias Die," and the page after that was "Love Potion for the Boy Next Door." That was where Bella Yaga came striding back to the table carrying the curled-up, dangling Thomas. Earwig hurriedly pushed the book back to the other side of the table and went back to thumping at the powder with both hands.

By suppertime, Earwig had seen about a quarter of the spells in the book, but not one of them seemed of any use to *her*. She thought for quite a while about a spell called "To Make a Skateboard Do Tricks," but although that sounded fun, there seemed nothing in it that would stop

Bella Yaga doing something awful to her if she tried it. And that was what she really needed, she thought, as she followed Bella Yaga down the hall to the kitchen. She needed to be safe from Bella Yaga before she could make her do anything.

To Earwig's surprise, the kitchen was an ordinary kitchen, quite warm and cozy, with the table laid for three and supper steaming on it. There was a large fish on a plate under the table, which Thomas hurried to eat. Earwig looked at the Mandrake. He was looming in a chair at the end of the table, reading a large leather book. He looked like an ordinary man in a bad temper. Even so, he did not look like a man who would have gotten supper ready.

"And what have the demons brought us

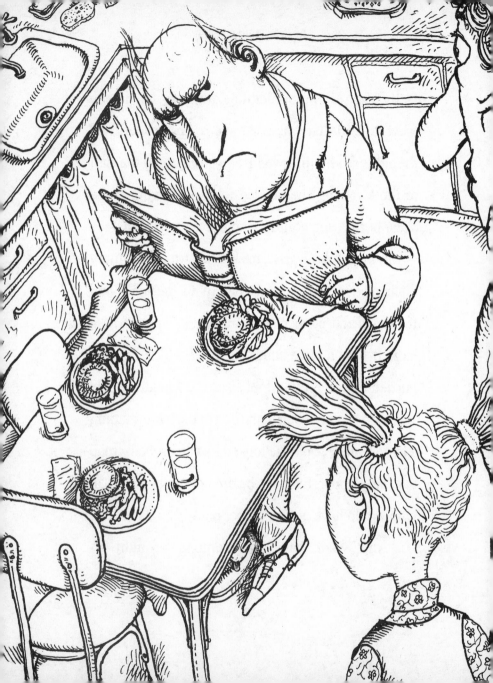

today?" Bella Yaga asked in the bright, wheedling voice she always seemed to use to the Mandrake.

"Pie and chips from Stoke-on-Trent station buffet," the Mandrake growled, without looking up.

"I hate station pie," said Bella Yaga.

The Mandrake looked up. His eyes were like dark pits. A spark of red fire glowed, deep down in each pit. "It's my favorite food," he said. The sparks in his eyes flickered and grew.

Earwig quite understood then why she was not to disturb the Mandrake. She was glad that he did not seem to notice she was there.

Chapter 3

For the next day or so, Earwig went about quietly finding out all she could about Thirteen Lime Avenue. It was a very strange place. For a start, there seemed no way to get out at the front. There was no front door on the inside. The place where it should have been was just bare wall. Earwig

could see the neat front garden out of the window
in her little bare bedroom, but when she tried to
open the window, she found there was no way to
open it. It was just glass built into the wall.

Earwig decided to see that as one more
challenge and find another way out. She could get
into the back garden easily enough. It was through
a door in the kitchen, and it was a riot of weeds.

Bella Yaga was always sending Earwig out there to pick nettles or briony berries or deadly nightshade. Every time, Earwig pushed her way through head-high nettles and thistles to a new place in the tangle of giant brambles around the edge, but all that happened was that she got scratched and stung.

"You won't get out that way!" Bella Yaga said, laughing meanly.

"Why not?" said Earwig.

"Because the Mandrake's got his demons guarding it, of course," Bella Yaga said.

Earwig nodded. That made another challenge. She began to see that she would have to make the Mandrake do what she wanted, too, and that would not be easy to do without disturbing him.

She went on exploring. The bungalow was much bigger inside than it had looked from the outside and there was a lot of it to explore. The door next to Earwig's room led to the bathroom. It was ordinary, like the kitchen. Earwig soon found that she was the only person who bothered to wash in it, or clean her teeth. As soon as she was sure, she took the bathroom over and pinned her snapshots of Custard and Mrs. Briggs to the cupboard door.

The door beyond the bathroom went into a huge room full of the kind of leather books the Mandrake read at supper. The door at the end of the hall, beside the kitchen door, opened into a dark place with a concrete floor that smelled—well, as if something had died in there. Earwig took a deep breath, held her nose, and tiptoed to the door at the other end. The place beyond there looked like a church, but there was a car—a little Citroën—parked in the middle between the pillars. There was no door to anywhere else from there. Earwig supposed it must be the garage. She backed out, rather annoyed.

Apart from these rooms and Bella Yaga's workroom, the kitchen was the only other room Earwig could find. When she went in there her first morning, she was surprised again at how ordinary it was. Thomas was sitting in the sun on the windowsill, with his front paws tucked under him, just like a normal cat. Bella Yaga was frying bacon and eggs at the stove.

"Watch carefully," Bella Yaga said to Earwig. "I shall expect you to cook breakfast in the future."

"Yes," said Earwig. "Where do you sleep? I can't find a door to your bedroom."

"Mind your own business," said Bella Yaga.

"What will you do to me if I don't?" Earwig asked.

She could tell that Bella Yaga had not expected that question. She looked rather taken aback and answered with the same threat she used on Thomas. "I shall give you worms." Then she seemed to feel she had better scare Earwig properly. She added, "Great big blue and purple wriggly worms. So take care, my girl!"

Earwig did not take care. She was quiet and dutiful in the workroom all day. Bella Yaga set her to chopping nettles, mashing poison berries, and slicing snakeskins into thin, thin strips. In the afternoons there were always things to count, grains of salt or newts' eyes. Earwig was annoyed again. In the first two days she only managed to look at the book of spells four times, and the only spell that seemed remotely useful was one headed "To Sharpen the Eyes at Night." While Earwig wondered how she might use that one, she kept a careful eye on what Bella Yaga did with the things Earwig had chopped and sliced for her. It looked interesting—and easy. Some of the things were boiled in the cauldron and then whipped into lotions with an old, rattly electric mixer. Others were carefully wrapped in small bundles inside a deadly nightshade leaf, which Bella Yaga then tied in special knots with the strips of snakeskin. Earwig would have liked to try doing that, too.

"The only thing wrong with magic is that it smells so awful," Earwig said to herself when she was in her own room at night. She sighed. Even the idea of doing a real spell herself did not quite make up for not living at St. Morwald's. She missed Custard quite dreadfully. And she was not used to sleeping alone at night. At St. Morwald's there had been dormitories with rows of beds. But the thing she missed most was not being able to go to the cook and ask for what she wanted for supper. "I used to be just like the Mandrake, I suppose." Earwig sighed. "Only he has demons to get him what he wants, lucky thing!"

The only thing that stopped her being really

46.

miserable was the cat, Thomas. Somehow he pushed her door open—though Earwig knew she had shut it tightly—and jumped on her bed, where he sat on her feet and purred. Earwig stroked him. His fur was soft and plushy and

quite clean, in spite of having been behind the cauldron all day. His purring, rumbling through her toes, was so comforting that Earwig talked to him a lot. Several times she made a mistake and called him Custard. That cheered her up so much that she got out her drawing things and made a very unkind drawing of Bella Yaga. She put in Bella Yaga's odd eyes and blue hair and purple lipstick, and she made her ribby face as ugly as possible. After that, she felt much better. In the morning, she pinned the picture up on the bathroom cupboard and felt better still.

Thomas came and sat on Earwig the next night, too. Earwig stroked him. Then she started to make a drawing of the Mandrake, as huge and frowning and horrible as she could make it. She put dots of red inside his eyes and added the horns—only they looked more like a donkey's ears. She would have liked to put in a demon or so, but she did not know what demons looked like, so she went back to making the Mandrake's face look horrible. But she kept being distracted in her drawing by a strange light on the wall of her room. It almost looked as if the wall was blushing, or there was a fire deep inside it.

"Whatever *is* that?" she said angrily, after she had made a mistake in the Mandrake's mouth the third time.

"It's the Mandrake," said Thomas. "His den's on the other side of this wall."

Earwig dropped her felt-tip pen and stared at the cat. His round, light-green eyes looked calmly back. "You—er—you speak!" she said.

"Of course," said Thomas. "Though not often. I think you should stop that drawing. It's beginning to disturb the Mandrake."

Earwig pushed her paper and pens

hurriedly under the covers. "Do you know about spells?" she asked.

"A fair amount. More than you do," said Thomas. "I've seen you looking in her book. The one you really want is near the end. Want me to show you?"

"Yes *please*!" said Earwig.

Chapter 4

"But just a moment," Earwig added. "How *can* the Mandrake's room be on the other side of this wall? That's the bathroom."

Thomas was in the middle of standing up and stretching his legs, in pairs. He looked at her over his sleek black shoulder. "Yes, I know," he said. "But it is, all the same." He finished stretching and sharpened his claws on the bedspread. "Coming?" he said and sprang to the floor.

Earwig pattered after him, out of her room and across the hall. The workroom door was locked. But Thomas stretched up and did some more claw-sharpening near the doorknob. The door quietly opened. Earwig fumbled the lights on and they crept inside.

"Oh, yucky!" Earwig cried out at the feel of the slime under her bare feet.

"Hush. You can lick them clean later." Thomas jumped onto the table and pawed the greasy little book. "Open it at the end and keep turning back until I tell you to stop," he said.

Earwig did so. She turned from "To Make a Plague of Worms," quickly, because Thomas began shuddering, to "A Thunderstorm to Spoil a Church Fete," and then to "A Spell to Make a Bus Come on Time," and "To Preserve the Body from All Magic," and—

"Hold it there," said Thomas. "That's ours. If we use that, she can't do a thing to either of us."

Earwig looked. The spell took up two pages in small writing. "But Custard—I mean, Thomas—it's got *hundreds* of things in it!"

"All of them are in this room somewhere and we've got all night," Thomas said. "Get going."

He sat in front of the book, tail curled around the front of his legs and twitching gently. "You'll need powdered rats' bones, newts' eyes, and well-sliced toad for the first stage. While you're doing those, you can start the henbane heating— you have to heat three hairs of a cat's tail in with it and mind you take them *gently*."

For quite half the night, Earwig slithered to and fro in the slime, working

far harder than she had ever worked for Bella Yaga during the day. Thomas sat bent over the book as if he were watching a mouse hole, calling out the next things the spell needed. "Belladonna now—that's the fourth bottle along, the one that's not as dusty as the others. Three drops in with the henbane." About halfway through, he said, "Familiar needed. That's all right. I'm here."

"What does that mean?" Earwig gasped. By this time she was pounding gunk with one hand and stirring a gooey green mixture with the other, as if her life depended on it. And perhaps it did, she thought. Bella Yaga was not going to forgive her for this if she found out.

"A familiar is a cat or other animal who is a witch's helper," Thomas said. "The animal needs to be close to the spell to make it work. And," he added smugly, "a black cat does that best of all."

"Then why do you always run away?" Earwig gasped, mixing and pounding. It was like trying to pat your head and rub your stomach at the same time.

"Because I don't like the kind of spells she does," said Thomas. "They make me feel as if someone is stroking me the wrong way. One drip of rose elixir into the green mix now."

Right near the end there was a nasty moment when Thomas read out, "Mix all together in a large bowl and say words."

"What words?" asked Earwig, bending over Thomas to look. There were no words written down in the book. After *say words*, the spell went on, *Spread resulting ointment over every part of your body*. "WHAT WORDS?" Earwig screamed. "It doesn't *say*!"

"Calm down!" said Thomas, who was looking a little twitchy himself. "They'll be words of binding. I've heard her use about six different words. I think I can remember—"

"You'd better remember, Custard—I mean, Thomas!" Earwig said. "After all this work I've done! Say them all. Every single one you've ever heard!"

"All right," Thomas said, flicking his tail irritably. "But only if you stop calling me Custard. And you'll have to say them after me exactly as I say them. You're the witch here, not me."

So Earwig stirred the mixture and listened carefully to all the strange words and noises Thomas made. She tried to say each one exactly the same way, which was not easy. Some of the sounds were very odd. But she thought the spell

was working. The mixture had been sort of pink when she tipped all the different parts into the bowl, but as she stirred and spoke, it turned colorless and smelled faintly of roses. She was very surprised that when Thomas stopped speaking, he toppled suddenly over on his back and writhed about the table with all his paws waving. "What's wrong?" she asked anxiously.

"Nothing!" Thomas said, in a kind of curdled purr. "It's just—it's just—some of the sounds were me swearing because I couldn't remember the words!"

Earwig realized he was laughing, in the way cats laugh. "Well, I just hope it works," she said. "What do I do now? Spread it all over me?"

Thomas sprang onto all four paws again rather quickly. "Yes, but you do me first," he said. "I've worked as hard as you did. And I've had enough of her giving me worms when she's annoyed."

This seemed fair enough. Earwig took two big fingerfuls of the colorless paste and rubbed them carefully into Thomas until his black coat was plastered wetly to his skin all over. Thomas crouched in a hump, with his fur sticking up in spikes. "*Yeurgh!*" he said, shaking a front paw disgustedly. "I hope it soaks in or something."

It seemed to soak in. By the time Earwig

was nearly through rubbing the mixture all over herself—very sparingly, because the paste got less and less horribly quickly—Thomas shook himself and was once more his sleek, plushy self. "That's better!" he said. He stuck up a back leg and washed, while Earwig wiped her dirty feet with a rag and spread the last of the paste over her soles and between her toes.

"Do you think it will work?" she said.

"*Flmph,*" said Thomas. His mouth was full of fur. "It had better work. I'm not going through all that again!"

"Neither am I!" said Earwig, when at last she yawned her way back to bed. It took ages to clear up and put all the things back so that Bella Yaga would not guess any of them had been used. After that she had to wash the slime off her feet and then clean the slimy footprints off the hall floor. Earwig nearly fell asleep on the floor while she was doing that.

And, naturally, it only seemed five minutes

after she had fallen asleep that Bella Yaga was

banging on her door and shouting.

"Get up, you lazy little beast! The Mandrake

wants his bacon and eggs."

"Tell him to get a demon to do it,"

Earwig growled.

"*What*?" screamed Bella Yaga.

"I'm *coming*!" Earwig shouted back. "And I'm not your slave!"

"That's what you think!" Bella Yaga yelled.

Chapter 5

Not surprisingly, Earwig was in a very bad temper that day. She grumbled under her breath while she worked in the workroom, and she grumbled out loud when she had to trudge out to the weed-garden to fetch nettles and hellebore. "I've had enough of being treated like a slave!"

she said. "And it's raining!" She trudged back and threw the wet plants down on the table.

"Don't do that!" snapped Bella Yaga. "I told you to put the plants in the cauldron, you useless little beast!"

"And I told you I'm not your slave!" Earwig snapped back. "I agreed to be your assistant and you agreed to teach me magic, and all you've done is work me half to death!"

"I did not agree to teach you magic!" Bella Yaga shouted. "I got you from St. Morwald's because I needed another pair of hands!"

"Then you're a cheat!" Earwig said. "You cheated Mrs. Briggs and you cheated me. You told Mrs. Briggs you were going to be my foster mother."

Bella Yaga glared at Earwig. She was in such a rage that her brown eye turned upward and her blue eye turned down. Earwig was quite frightened and wondered if she had gone too far. But all Bella Yaga did was to slap Earwig around the head so hard that her ears rang. "Foster mother indeed!" she said, laughing angrily. "Go and put more fuel under the cauldron. Now. Or I'll give you worms."

Earwig went giddily over to the mound of sludge where the green flames were and piled sticks under the cauldron. When her head had cleared a little, she said, "Well? Are you going to teach me magic or not?"

"Of course not," said Bella Yaga. "You're

only my spare pair of hands."

Right! Earwig thought. *That does it!*

She seethed with rage for the rest of the morning, but she took care to seethe quietly so that Bella Yaga would not see how angry she was. Lunch was the specially nice shepherd's pie that the cook at St. Morwald's used to make Earwig as a special treat. The Mandrake had made his demons fetch it because he liked it, too. Earwig could scarcely believe it when she recognized it. She stared at her plate and could hardly eat for anger and homesickness.

After lunch, Bella Yaga gathered up all the spells from the last few days, put each one carefully in a plastic bag, and packed all the bags in a shopping basket. She unhooked her red hat from the hall and put it on her head. "I'm off to deliver these to my customers," she said.

In spite of being so angry, Earwig was interested enough to ask, "Do you go on a broomstick?"

"Certainly not," said Bella Yaga. "All my customers are very respectable. They belong to Friends of the Earth and the Mothers Union. They'd have fits if their neighbors saw me arrive on a broomstick! Now stop asking stupid questions and get the floor in here clean. I want to be able to eat my dinner off it when I come back."

Earwig watched Bella Yaga open the blank wall at the end of the hall just as if it was a front

door and go out. As soon as the wall slammed
shut, Earwig raced back to the workroom, calling
for Thomas.

"What is it?" Thomas asked grumpily,

struggling out from one of the mixing bowls. "I was asleep. The only time I get any peace is when she goes out."

"Yes, I know," Earwig said. "But just help me for five minutes. What's a spell for giving someone another pair of hands?"

Thomas's foot stopped halfway to irritably scratching his chin. "*What* a good idea!" he said respectfully. "Let's look in her book."

The only spell in the book that was anything like what Earwig had in mind was called "To Make Extra Growth on a Person's Body." "Do you think it might do?" she asked Thomas.

"Just about," Thomas said, crouched over the page. "The real difficulty is how to get a hair of her head to put in the image. She won't let you near her hair if she can help it."

"I'll get one somehow," Earwig said grimly. "She keeps saying she wants another pair of hands. She's going to get them if it kills me!"

Earwig worked feverishly for the next hour. The spell told her to make an image of the person out of all sorts of unpleasant things. Then you made the extra bits you wanted out of bats' wings and beeswax and stuck those on, with Thomas standing by as familiar. The thing that made the spell work was a hair from the head of the person you were working on, wrapped around the image.

Earwig enjoyed making a model of Bella Yaga. She ran to the bathroom from time to time to look at her picture, to make sure she was getting it ugly enough. But she had trouble with the spare pair of hands. They were so tiny. She had to roll them up and start again three times. Then when at last she got them right, she could not decide on the best place to put them.

"Do you think on her elbows?" she asked Thomas.

"On her knees?" Thomas suggested. "She—" He stopped and stood up in an arch with all his fur on end. "Hide it! Quick! She's coming back!"

Earwig could not hear anything, but she knew animals' ears were far better than humans'. She did not argue. She stuck the two tiny hands on anywhere in order not to lose them. She scooped up the image—and a big screwdriver with it, because of another idea she had had—and ran with it all to her bedroom. She pushed the model and the screwdriver under her pillow and ran back to the workroom. There was just time to get a broom and start pushing it about before Bella Yaga came in.

"Do you call that floor clean?" Bella Yaga said. "You don't get any supper unless you do better than that, you lazy creature!"

Earwig had to sweep and scrape and scrub for the rest of the day. But she was so busy thinking of ways to get a hair from Bella Yaga's head that she hardly noticed what she was doing. She thought if she could only find Bella Yaga's bedroom, it would be easy. There would be a comb or a hairbrush on the dressing table and there would be hair in those. Bella Yaga never tidied anything up.

By suppertime the floor was almost clean, but not quite. Bella Yaga grinned meanly. "You can go to your bedroom and have bread and cheese for supper there," she said. "That might teach you not to be so lazy in the future!"

Earwig ran to her room, hoping to see the demon who brought the bread and cheese. But it was a little disappointing. *Something* certainly came into the room. There was a whirling wind and a feeling of hotness. But all Earwig *saw* was a plate of Ploughman's Lunch from the pub down the road, which suddenly appeared in the middle of her bed, and the whirling stopped as soon as she saw it.

"Are you there?" said Earwig. But nothing was.

After she had eaten the Ploughman's Lunch—it was quite filling, with two kinds of pickle and a hardboiled egg as well as cheese and French bread—Earwig thoughtfully took the screwdriver from under her pillow. She knelt down by the wall that was supposed to have the bathroom on the other side and started to make a hole in it with the screwdriver. Thomas had said that the Mandrake's room was on the other side. It stood to reason that Bella Yaga's room was there, too. So Earwig bored and twiddled and scraped with the screwdriver, until she felt the end of it come loose into air on the other side of the wall. Then, very slowly and gently, scarcely daring to breathe, she pulled the screwdriver out and put her eye to the hole.

A hotness blew in her eye. She had to wipe plaster dust out of it before she could look again. When she had, she found she was not looking at a bedroom. Nor was it the bathroom. It seemed to be a kind of study through there, painted in black and gold and red. The huge figure of the Mandrake was nearby, sitting at some kind of desk. Beyond him was a whirling, writhing Something. Earwig could only see bits of the something, but she was fairly sure it was a demon. And if it *was* a demon, she knew she did not want to see a demon ever again. She took

her eye away and plugged up the hole with the screwdriver.

"Bother!" she said. This did not get her any nearer to getting hold of one of Bella Yaga's hairs. She squatted on her heels, thinking. After a bit, still thinking, she got up and went to the bathroom and looked at the wall there. Sure enough, there was a little crumbly hole and she could just see the tip of the screwdriver sticking through it.

"I don't understand magic," Earwig said. "She's going to *have* to teach me about it."

Chapter 6

Next morning, Bella Yaga was screaming as usual. "Wake up! Hurry up! The Mandrake wants fried bread for breakfast today!"

Earwig shot out of bed, shot into her clothes, and shot to the hall to go to the bathroom. There she came to a dead stop and stood staring at

Bella Yaga's red hat, hanging on its peg.

"Of course!" she said. "I bet there's a hair in that hat!"

Quickly, she unhooked the hat and, sure enough, there were two hairs, curly and blue-purple, clinging to the hatband inside. Earwig picked them off and raced to the bathroom, where she hid them in her sponge bag.

"Hurry up!" screamed Bella Yaga.

You wait! Earwig thought. She hurried to the kitchen and put some slices of bread in the frying pan. The bread drank all the fat in the pan and then it burned, in spite of Earwig pouring in what felt like a gallon more fat as it cooked.

The Mandrake stared at the plate of dry black slices. "What is this?" He turned his eyes to Earwig. She saw the red sparks lighting up in them.

"I've never done fried bread before," she said. "Isn't it right?"

"No," said the Mandrake. The burning pits of his eyes turned to Bella Yaga. "Why didn't you teach her how?"

Bella Yaga went pale. "Well, I—er—anyone can cook fried bread."

"Wrong," said the Mandrake. "Don't let it disturb me again." He waved his hand. There was a sort of wavering in the air over his left shoulder. A sweet voice spoke out of nowhere.

"How can I serve my hideous master today?"

"Don't be rude," growled the Mandrake. "You can take this food away and get me some real fried bread from the scout camp in Epping Forest."

"Yes, ghastly master," the voice said. The wobbling air whirled. In the time it took Earwig to blink, the burned bread had gone and there were golden crisp slices on the plate instead. The Mandrake grunted and began to eat, then, in terrible, powerful silence. Bella Yaga kept very quiet, too. Earwig saw that Thomas had crawled away to hide behind the wastebucket under the sink, so she wisely said nothing either. Breakfast seemed to go on for a year.

When it was over at last, Bella Yaga hurried Earwig to the workroom. "How *dare* you disturb the Mandrake like that!" she scolded. "You nearly had me in bad trouble!"

"Well, you should try to teach me things instead of just making me do them," Earwig said.

"Don't give me silly excuses!" said Bella Yaga. "You're here to work. I told you I need another pair of hands."

You'll get them, Earwig thought fiercely.

They started work. When enough time had passed to make it seem likely, Earwig said, "I need to go to the toilet."

"Anything to annoy me!" said Bella Yaga. "All right. You can have exactly two minutes. Any longer and I give you worms."

Earwig raced away to the bathroom and collected the two hairs from her sponge bag. She raced to her bedroom. In a terrible hurry, she lifted up the pillow, planted the two hairs on the little image of Bella Yaga, and raced back to the bathroom to flush the toilet. She sped back to the workroom.

There was a terrible howl as she opened the door. Thomas shot between Earwig's legs and dived into her bedroom out of sight.

"What have you done?" Bella Yaga was shrieking. "You wicked girl, what have you *done*?"

Earwig put both hands over her mouth in order not to laugh out loud. She had not noticed where she had stuck on the extra hands. She had been in too much of a hurry. One had ended up stuck to Bella Yaga's forehead. It flapped there, with its fingers opening and shutting in front of Bella Yaga's eyes. As Earwig looked, its finger and thumb found Bella Yaga's nose and pinched. Bella Yaga howled and spun around. The other hand, to Earwig's great pleasure, was stuck to the back of Bella Yaga's tweed

skirt like a tail. That was pinching her, too.

"Whad hab you dud?" Bella Yaga yelled again, trying to wrench the finger and thumb away from her nose.

"Given you an extra pair of hands," Earwig said. "Just like you said you wanted."

"Ooh!" howled Bella Yaga. "I'll gib you wurbs!"

Earwig found herself being pushed and hurried backward. It was like being swept by an invisible broom. The pushing landed her inside her bedroom and shut the door on her with a slam. Earwig heard the lock click and knew she was locked in, this time. She turned around and saw Thomas standing on her bed, looped into a hoop, with his fur on end and his eyes staring.

"Stay there!" Bella Yaga screamed from outside. "Stay there with wurbs!"

Thomas gave a long and trembling howl and dived under the covers of Earwig's bed. There he crawled and pushed and scrambled until he was a small very flat hump right down at the very end.

"You don't need to hide," Earwig said to him. "We did that spell. She can't hurt us."

But Thomas clearly had no faith in the spell at all. He stayed where he was and would not speak or move, even when Earwig prodded him. She sighed and sat on her bed to see what would happen about the worms.

After a minute or so, the image of Bella Yaga flew out from under the pillow and flopped on the floor. Earwig saw that the two little hands had come loose. She picked up the image and tried to stick the hands back on. She tried them in several places, but nothing seemed to make them stick. Earwig sighed again, because she knew that Bella

Yaga had somehow broken the spell completely.

Then the worms arrived. They appeared in a big wriggling bundle out of nowhere and fell to the floor by Earwig's feet. Earwig pulled her feet out of their way and stared down at them. There seemed to be at least a hundred of them. They were the size of earthworms, and as Bella Yaga had promised, they were blue and purple and very wriggly. The wriggliness, Earwig saw, was because the worms were not happy out on the bare floor. Some of them were trying to wriggle down the cracks in the floorboards to get out of the daylight.

"Our spell works," Earwig told the hump that was Thomas. "The worms are on the floor, not doing any harm at all."

The hump refused to move or speak.

"Scaredy-cat!" said Earwig. "You're worse than Custard."

But since Thomas still refused to speak or come out, Earwig sat and thought about the worms. They did not worry her at all, for being worms. But something worried her. After a while, she knew what it was. Those worms were supposed to be inside her. If Bella Yaga found out they were

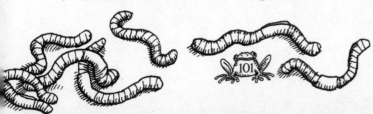

on the floor instead, she would know that Earwig and Thomas worked the spell to keep themselves safe. And then Bella Yaga would break that spell at once.

Earwig wondered how to hide the worms. The only hiding place in the room was inside the bed, and since Thomas was so scared of worms, that was not kind. But—Earwig's eyes went to the screwdriver still sticking out of the wall. That hole she had made was exactly the right size to take a worm. Bella Yaga never seemed to go near the bathroom, so the worms could creep under the bathmat and stay hidden there until Bella Yaga decided to let Earwig out. Then she could put them in a bucket and take them out into the weed-garden, where they would be happier.

Earwig got up and pulled the screwdriver out of the wall. Then she picked up the nearest blue wriggling worm and coaxed it into the hole. The worm went in eagerly. It really hated being out on the floor. As soon as it was through, Earwig picked up the next, and the next. She put worm after worm through the wall, feeling as if she was doing a good deed. Everyone was much happier like this, and Bella Yaga need never know.

She was feeding the last worm through the hole when Thomas crawled out from under the bedclothes. "What are you doing?" he said.

"Sending the worms to hide in the bathroom," Earwig explained.

"No!" yowled Thomas and went back under the bedclothes like a rat up a drainpipe.

"Honestly, Custard—I mean, Thomas!" Earwig said as she let go of the last worm's tail. "Anyone would think—"

The wall turned red-hot.

Earwig got to the other side of the room quicker even than Thomas had got down inside the bed. There was a growling from behind the red-hot wall that very quickly rose to a howling and then a roaring. Earwig covered her ears. As she did, most of the wall vanished and the Mandrake stormed through. He was alight with black fire and taller than ever. His eyes were red pits of rage. Dark fire streamed backward from the horns on his head.

Earwig found herself crouched under her bed without knowing how she had got there.

"Worms!" bellowed the Mandrake. "I'LL GIVE HER WORMS!"

From under the bed Earwig saw his huge feet, which now seemed to have claws on them, make smoking holes in the floor as he marched across her bedroom and out through the wall beside the door. A roaring and rushing filled the air behind him. Peeping from where she crouched, Earwig saw scaly paws, ratty tails, slimy hooves, horny wing tips, and many queerer things that were parts of the host of demons following the Mandrake. She did not try to see all of any of them. In fact some of them made her hide her face in her hands.

There was a huge crash as the Mandrake walked through the workroom wall. There was a noise like a thunderstorm. Earwig heard Bella Yaga shrieking, "It wasn't me! It wasn't me!" Then she heard Bella Yaga shrieking angry spells. Then there was a crashing, and Bella Yaga was just shrieking. Earwig saw flickers of green and black light.

Then there was quiet. It was not a good quiet. Earwig stayed where she was. She did not move, nor take her hands from her face, even when she heard her bedroom door open.

"Come out," said the Mandrake.

Earwig crawled out, very slowly. To her surprise, there were no burned patches in the floor and no kind of holes in the walls. The Mandrake was standing in the doorway looking like an ordinary man in a bad mood, except for the little red sparks in the middle of his eyes.

"She gave you worms," he said.

"Yes," said Earwig, "and I put them into the bathroom to hide. It was a mistake."

"Magic worms go through into a magic place," the Mandrake said. "They went into my den. She won't do that to you again. You won't do that again. I've told her she's to make you a proper assistant and teach you properly. I don't like being disturbed."

"Thank you," said Earwig. "Could you make her send me to school tomorrow, too, when term starts? I need to see my friend Custard."

"Maybe," said the Mandrake. He walked across to the wall where Earwig had made the hole.

"The bungalow will be much more peaceful if I'm out all day," Earwig pointed out quickly.

"I'll think about it," said the Mandrake. He walked into the wall and vanished.

"Oh well," said Earwig. She turned around and dug Thomas out from under the bedclothes. He lay heavy and soft in her arms. Earwig put her face on his fur, and he began to purr. Earwig smiled. She thought about what had just happened. "You know," she told Thomas, "if I work things out right, we ought to be able to make both of them behave just the way we want them to."

She carried Thomas across the hall to the workroom. Bella Yaga, looking red and

harried, was picking up broken glass and bits of mixing bowls. She turned her blue eye nastily in Earwig's direction. Earwig said quickly, before Bella Yaga could speak, "Please, I've come for my first magic lesson."

Bella Yaga sighed angrily. "All right," she said. "You win—for now. But I wish I knew how you did it!"

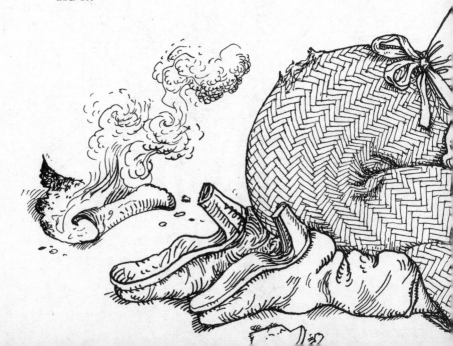

A year went by.

Earwig sighed happily as she woke up and tried to get her toes from under fat Thomas. Everyone in her new home now did exactly what she told them to do. It was almost better than the orphanage. The Mandrake had even taken to calling her Dearwig. When Earwig asked him to tell his demons to fetch her breakfast, the demons fetched it at once. They were beginning to do what Earwig told them to do without her having to ask the Mandrake first. Yesterday they had brought her the breakfast menu from the best hotel in town. Earwig picked it up and studied it.

Breakfast in bed with kippers, she thought, or scrambled eggs, or

why not both? While she was wondering whether or not to have yogurt as well, she remembered the only sad thing in her life. Nothing would induce Custard to come and visit her. He was much too afraid of the Mandrake. Still, she thought, deciding to have mixed grill after all, she could work on Custard just as she had worked on her new household.

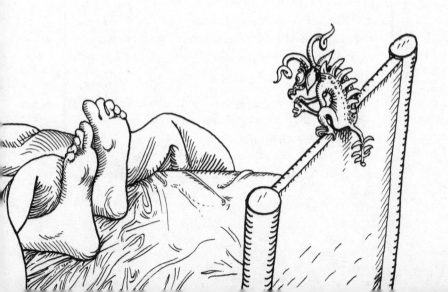

Paul O. Zelinsky's exquisite illustrations are admired by fans worldwide and have established him as one of the top illustrators in children's book publishing. He illustrated *Z Is for Moose*, by Kelly Bingham, and *Doodler Doodling*, by Rita Golden Gelman. *Rapunzel*, his retelling of the classic fairy tale, won the Caldecott Medal in 1998. He received Caldecott Honors for *Rumpelstiltskin* and for his illustrations in *Hansel and Gretel*, by Rika Lesser, and *Swamp Angel*, by Anne Isaacs. Paul O. Zelinsky lives in Brooklyn, New York. www.paulozelinsky.com